I Can Read! READING WITH HELP 2

KONG
THE 8TH WONDER OF THE WORLD™

MEET KONG AND ANN

Adapted by Jennifer Frantz

Illustrations by Peter Bollinger and Robert Papp

Based on a Motion Picture Screenplay by Fran Walsh & Philippa Boyens & Peter Jackson

Based on a Story by Merian C. Cooper and Edgar Wallace

HarperCollins*Publishers*

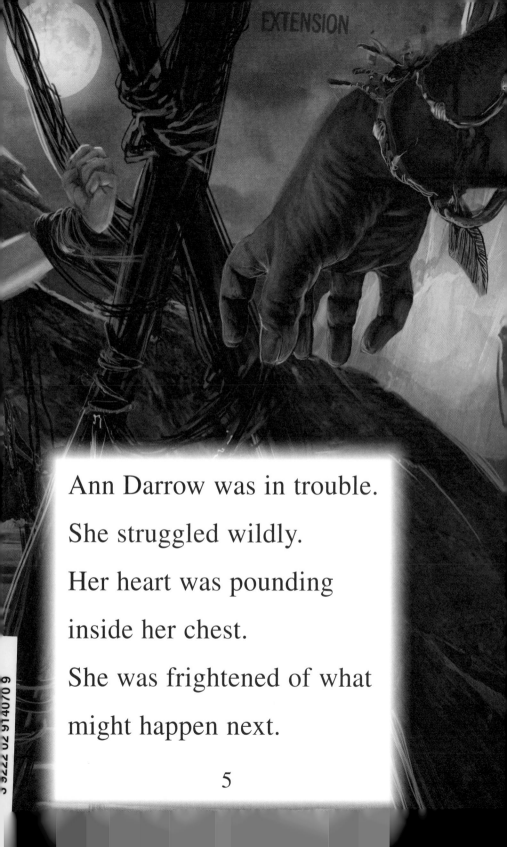

Ann Darrow was in trouble.

She struggled wildly.

Her heart was pounding
inside her chest.

She was frightened of what
might happen next.

5

Ann tried to remember how
she had gotten into this mess.
One minute she was a stage performer
in New York City . . .
the next she was fighting
for her life on an uncharted island.

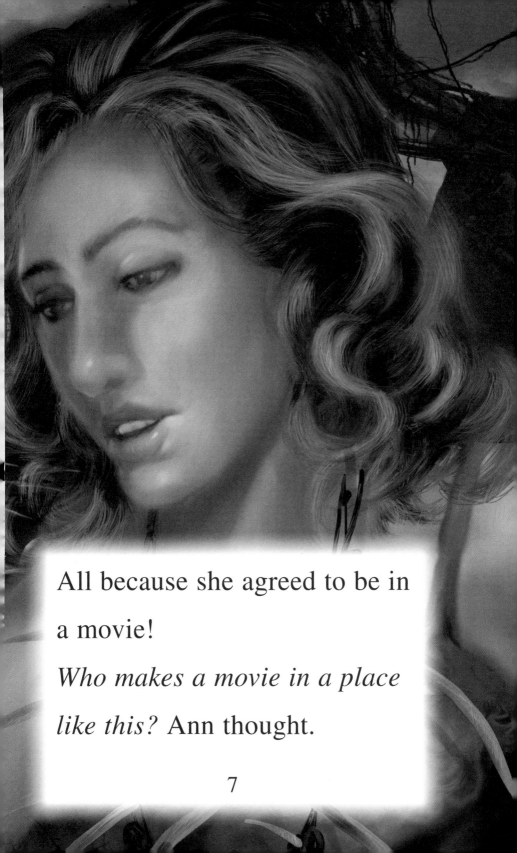

All because she agreed to be in a movie!

Who makes a movie in a place like this? Ann thought.

Suddenly the ground shook.

Branches snapped loudly.

Ann heard a roar through the trees.

What terrible creature was coming for her?

Just then it appeared—
a giant gorilla.

His name was Kong, and he
was taller than a house!

10

Kong's large, powerful eyes
glared at Ann.

Then he snatched her up
in one huge, leathery hand.

Ann was like a rag doll

clutched by the giant hand

of the beast.

Kong raced through the
jungle with Ann.
She was powerless.

13

They reached a rocky clearing, and the giant gorilla stopped. Kong held Ann up to his face. Ann looked back.

14 14

There was something about her that interested the beast.
But not for long.

Suddenly the giant gorilla flipped Ann upside down.

A necklace the island's inhabitants had put on her slipped over her head and fell to the ground.

It landed on a pile of necklaces just like it.

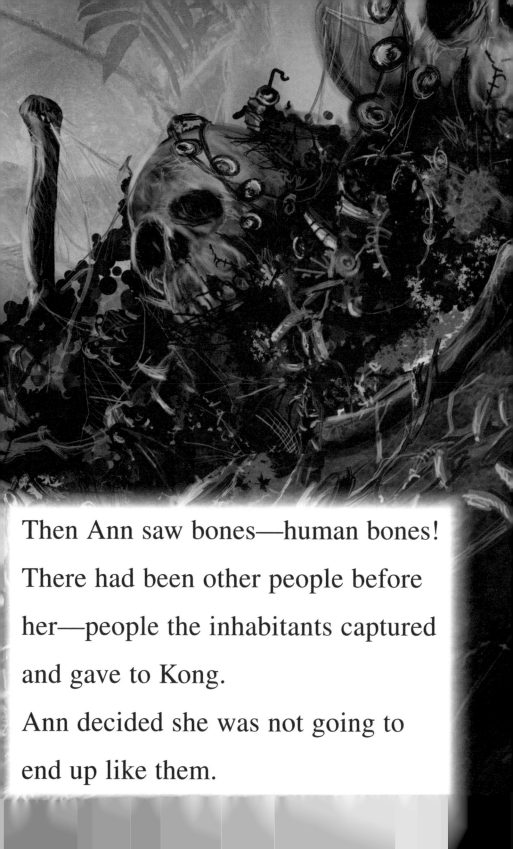

Then Ann saw bones—human bones!
There had been other people before
her—people the inhabitants captured
and gave to Kong.
Ann decided she was not going to
end up like them.

Ann took a deep breath and jumped from Kong's hand. She landed with a thud on the rocky ground below.

Her body was sore from the fall, but Ann could not rest now. She picked herself up and ran off toward the jungle.

She did not get far.

Kong slammed his huge fist

on the ground.

Ann tumbled and fell.

The beast seemed to think

this was a game.

Ann pretended to fall,

over and over again.

She wanted to keep the beast happy.

After many falls, Ann was bruised

and tired.

But she had not given up yet.
Ann dashed away from Kong,
scrambling onto a fallen log.

Then Ann heard a snarl.

She could not believe her eyes.

It was a gigantic dinosaur!

25

Kong approached the terrible dinosaur.

The giants locked into battle.

The dinosaur fought violently, but Kong would not give up.

He was protecting Ann.

Before long, Kong defeated the dinosaur.

Kong had saved Ann!
Frustrated, she gave up
hope of escape.

Kong looked down at Ann,
then scooped her up gently.
Ann saw kindness in his eyes.
She was exhausted, but she was
no longer afraid.

Together, they traveled for a
long time.

At last, Ann and the beast
reached the top of a tall mountain.

From the mountaintop, there was a full view of Skull Island below. From up there, the island looked beautiful.

Later Ann realized that Kong was
the king of Skull Island,
and that he wanted to share his
world with Ann.
The two sat quietly, watching
the sunset.

Dear Parent:
Your child's love of reading starts here!

Every child learns to read in a different way and at his or her own speed. Some go back and forth between reading levels and read favorite books again and again. Others read through each level in order. You can help your young reader improve and become more confident by encouraging his or her own interests and abilities. From books your child reads with you to the first books he or she reads alone, there are I Can Read Books for every stage of reading:

SHARED READING
Basic language, word repetition, and whimsical illustrations, ideal for sharing with your emergent reader

BEGINNING READING
Short sentences, familiar words, and simple concepts for children eager to read on their own

READING WITH HELP
Engaging stories, longer sentences, and language play for developing readers

READING ALONE
Complex plots, challenging vocabulary, and high-interest topics for the independent reader

ADVANCED READING
Short paragraphs, chapters, and exciting themes for the perfect bridge to chapter books

I Can Read Books have introduced children to the joy of reading since 1957. Featuring award-winning authors and illustrators and a fabulous cast of beloved characters, I Can Read Books set the standard for beginning readers.

A lifetime of discovery begins with the magical words "I Can Read!"

Visit www.icanread.com for information
on enriching your child's reading experience.

King Kong: Meet Kong and Ann

© 2005 Universal Studios Licensing LLLP. Universal Studios' King Kong movie © Universal Studios. Kong The 8th Wonder of the World™ Universal Studios. All Rights Reserved. No part of this book may be used or reproduced in any manner whatsoever without written permission except in the case of brief quotations embodied in critical articles and reviews. Printed in the United States of America. For information address HarperCollins Children's Books, a division of HarperCollins Publishers, 1350 Avenue of the Americas, New York, NY 10019. www.harperchildrens.com

Library of Congress Catalog Card Number: 2005928974
ISBN-10: 0-06-077300-6 (pbk.) — ISBN-13: 978-0-06-077300-7 (pbk.)

1 2 3 4 5 6 7 8 9 10   ❖   First Edition